I Don't Like Salad!

Tony Ross

Andersen Press · London

The Little Princess raced into the kitchen.
"It's lunchtime and I'm hungry!"
Tap! Tap! Tap! The Chef was chopping
ingredients at top speed.
"Maybe I'll have pasta," pondered the
Little Princess, "maybe rice, maybe 'tatoes.
It'll be something yummy!"

The Chef kissed his fingers, then proudly presented her with a plate of salad. *"Voilà!"*

"Ugh!"

The Little Princess prodded a tomato with her fork.

"What's that?"

The Chef sniffed.

"It's delicious *salade du chef*."

"Yuk!" groaned the Little Princess.

"Perhaps some mayonnaise?"
he suggested, heading for the fridge.
The Little Princess spotted
her chance. Quick as a flash,
she tipped the salad into her lap.

When the Chef got back to the table,
he gasped.
"Where is it?"

"All gone!"
smiled the Little Princess. "Can I have my pudding now?"

The Little Princess grabbed her pudding and scrambled outside, spilling bits of her lunch on the way.

"That looked yucky!" she grinned. "Especially the tomato."

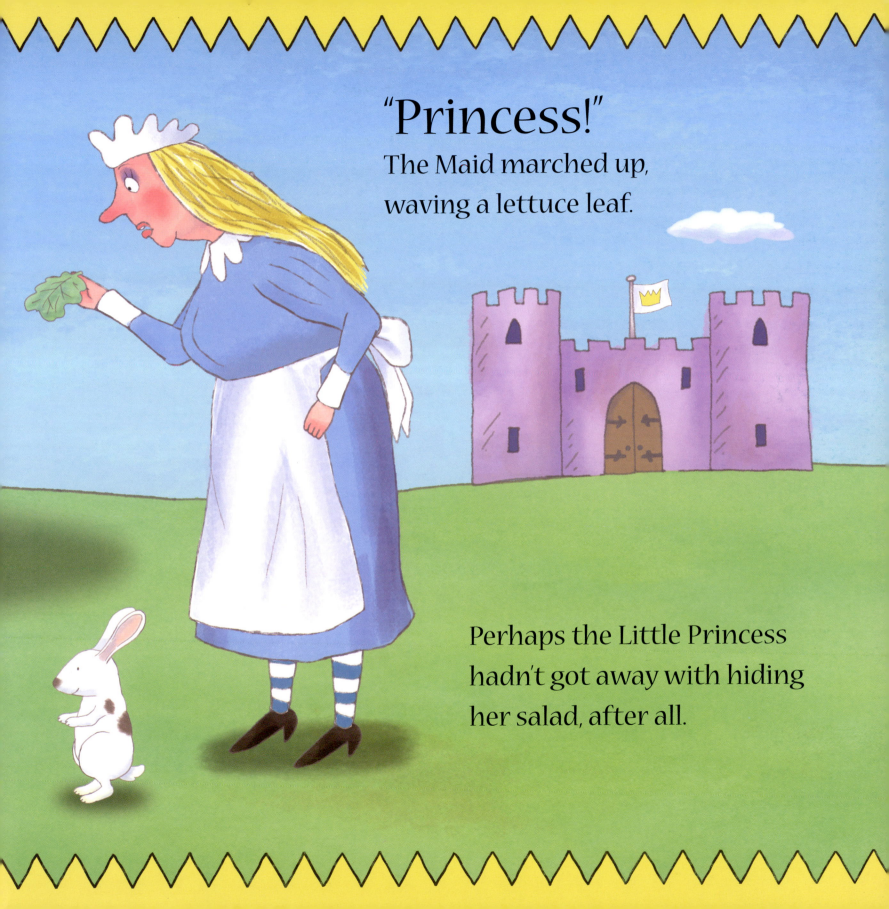

"Princess!"
The Maid marched up,
waving a lettuce leaf.

Perhaps the Little Princess
hadn't got away with hiding
her salad, after all.

The Chef gestured at the salad on the
kitchen table. "You see, I find it everywhere!"
"Now, love," said the Queen. "You mustn't waste good food."
"You do not like my cooking?" asked the Chef.

The Little Princess frowned. "It's not cooking, it's raw!"

"But it's good food," said the King. "Grown especially by the Gardener."

The Maid thought for a moment.

"Maybe she should see where it comes from?"

"So," said the Gardener. "You don't like my salad?"

The Little Princess shook her head.

"Well, I love it," he chuckled. "But then I grow everything myself."

The Gardener held out a handful of tiny seeds for her to look at.
"How do the plants fit in there?" gasped the Little Princess.
The Gardener smiled wisely. "The wonder of Mother Nature."

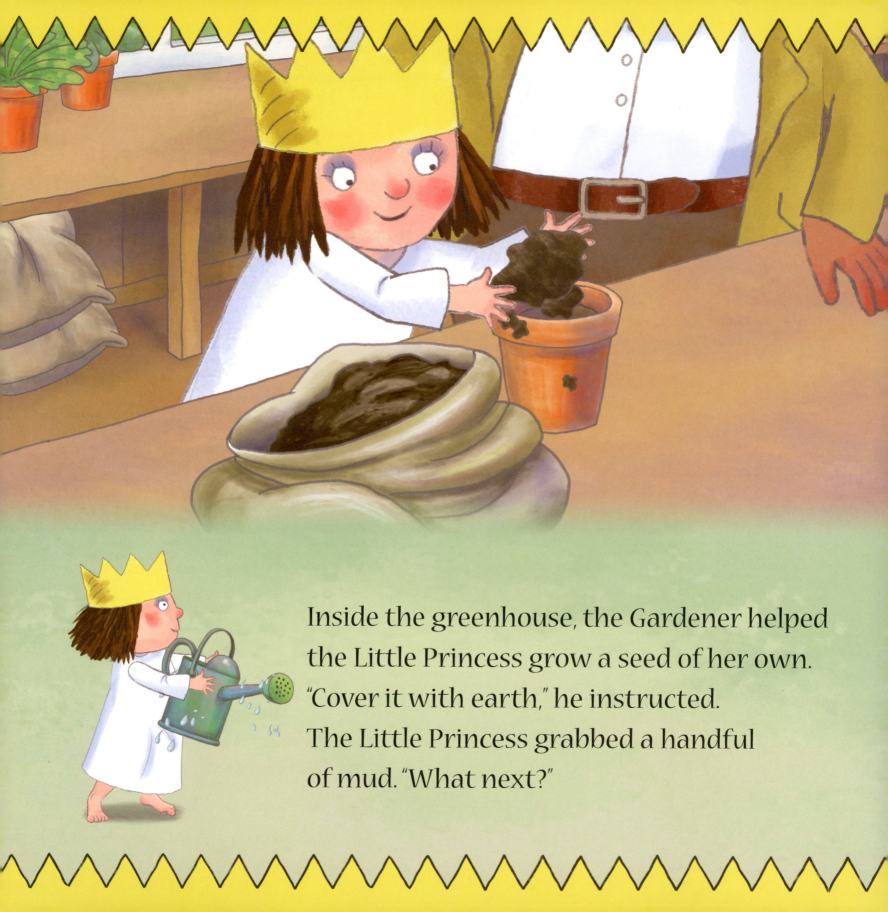

Inside the greenhouse, the Gardener helped
the Little Princess grow a seed of her own.
"Cover it with earth," he instructed.
The Little Princess grabbed a handful
of mud. "What next?"

"Now water it." The Gardener laughed as water sprinkled everywhere. "And… wait."

The Little Princess sat by her
pot for ages, but nothing sprouted.
"Plants take a long time to grow," she decided at bedtime.
After a week of waiting, the Little Princess nearly gave up.
"I think my seed was empty," she told the Maid.

Then one morning, it finally happened.
"It's growing," cried the Little Princess.
"It's growing!"

The Gardener was summoned
to examine the tiny green shoot.
"It's a fine specimen,"
he announced.

The Little Princess didn't reply.
She was too busy hugging
her pot.

The tiny shoot quickly grew into a great big tomato plant.
The Little Princess rushed out to visit it every morning.
"I love tomatoes now," she decided. "But just to play with."

The Little Princess and the plant became best friends.

Sometimes they wheeled out the pram and went for a walk.

Sometimes they went for a swim.

Sometimes, the Little Princess
chose stories for them to read.
(Their favourite was about a
princess and a pea.)

And sometimes
the pair went
dancing together!

One lunchtime, the Little Princess popped in extra early
to say hello to her plant. "Huh?"
The Chef was standing in the greenhouse, holding
a pair of scissors!
The Little Princess screamed. "What are you doing to Tommy?"

"The tomatoes are ripe," spluttered the Chef.
"Perfect for my salad."

"They ... are ... NOT ... for eating!"

As soon as the Chef had been shooed away, the Little Princess gently watered Tommy. "I'm going to look after him for ever and ever," she decided.

Ker-splat!
The plant's roundest, reddest tomato dropped onto the floor!

The Little Princess shrieked for the Gardener,
but he didn't seem surprised.
"They get so ripe they just fall off the plant," he explained.

The Little Princess tried propping up Tommy
with the castle's comfiest cushions.

Ker-pl**op!** It was no use. Two more tomatoes
tumbled into the Little Princess's hands.

"Princess?" The Queen stood in the doorway. "We do not waste good food."

The Chef stepped forward and gently took the tomatoes. "Thank you."

The Little Princess nodded sadly. She needed a hug.

Dinner was served.

"Some for you, Princess?" asked the Chef.

"The tomatoes are so juicy!"

The Little Princess hid her face in her hands.

The King and Queen tucked in.

"Best toms I've ever eaten," marvelled the King. "She's so clever!"

The Little Princess looked up.

"You looked after the plant so well, it has grown really tasty tomatoes," said the Queen. "They're presents for you."

It was hard to say no to a present. The Little Princess gulped and tried a bite of tomato. "Er… nice!"
Suddenly she noticed some tiny pips on her plate.
"Those are the seeds," explained the King.

"Seeds?" The Little Princess squealed with delight.
"I can grow some more!" Now everyone could enjoy…

…salade de la Princesse!